Laura Ingalls Wilder
Park and Museum

Burr Oak, Iowa

A
LITTLE HOUSE
CHRISTMAS
TREASURY

Festive Holiday Stories

Laura Ingalls Wilder

ILLUSTRATED BY GARTH WILLIAMS

HARPERCOLLINS*PUBLISHERS*

HarperCollins®, ▰®, and Little House®
are trademarks of HarperCollins Publishers Inc.

A Little House Christmas Treasury
Text copyright © 1994, 2005 by HarperCollins Publishers Inc.
Illustrations copyright © 1953 by Garth Williams

Little House in the Big Woods text copyright 1932, 1960
Little House Heritage Trust
Little House on the Prairie text copyright 1935, 1963
Little House Heritage Trust
On the Banks of Plum Creek text copyright 1937, 1965
Little House Heritage Trust
Farmer Boy text copyright 1933, 1961
Little House Heritage Trust
The Long Winter text copyright 1940, 1968
Little House Heritage Trust
These Happy Golden Years text copyright 1943, 1971
Little House Heritage Trust

Library of Congress Cataloging-in-Publication Data
Wilder, Laura Ingalls, 1867–1957.
   A little house Christmas treasury : festive holiday stories / by Laura Ingalls Wilder ; illustrated by Garth Williams.
       p.   cm.—(Little house)
   Summary: A collection of stories and music which describe the experiences of a pioneer girl and her family as they celebrate various Christmases in the Big Woods in Wisconsin, on the prairie in Indian Territory, and on the banks of Plum Creek.
   ISBN 0-06-076918-1
   1. Wilder, Laura Ingalls, 1867–1957—Juvenile fiction. [1. Wilder, Laura Ingalls, 1867–1957—Fiction. 2. Christmas—Fiction. 3. Frontier and pioneer life—Fiction. 4. Family life—Fiction.] I. Williams, Garth, ill. II. Title. III. Series.
PZ7.W6461Lh 2005   2004054331
[Fic]—dc22   CIP
                                                                            AC

2   3   4   5   6   7   8   9   10
❖

Contents

O nce upon a time, a little girl named Laura Ingalls lived in a log cabin in the Big Woods of Wisconsin with her Pa, her Ma, her big sister Mary, and her baby sister Carrie. Laura had many adventures as she traveled west across the prairie with her family in their covered wagon, and when Laura was grown, she wrote about these adventures in the Little House books. Some of the most wonderful stories in these books are those that tell of the merry Christmas *celebrations in the little houses in the*

Big Woods of Wisconsin, on the Kansas

prairie, on the banks of beautiful Plum

Creek in Minnesota, at Almanzo's family

home in Malone, New York, and finally,

in the town of De Smet in the Dakota

Territory during the happy golden years

when Laura and Almanzo fell in love.

Here are the Christmas stories from

those long-ago days, gathered together

in one very special holiday storybook.

Merry Christmas to all!

It's wintertime in the Big Woods of Wisconsin, and a little log cabin deep in the woods is almost covered with snow. Inside the cabin, a little girl named Laura Ingalls is very excited, because Christmas is almost here! Laura is only four years old, but she's big enough to help her Pa, her Ma, and her big sister Mary get the little house ready for Christmas visitors. It's very cold and snowy outside, but Laura and Mary know that Santa Claus will be coming soon with all sorts of Christmas treasures.

Christmas
in the
Big Woods

Christmas

CHRISTMAS WAS COMING.

The little log house was almost buried in snow. Great drifts were banked against the walls and windows, and in the morning when Pa opened the door, there was a wall of snow as high as Laura's head. Pa took the shovel and shoveled it away, and then he shoveled a path to the barn, where the horses and the cows were snug and warm in their stalls.

The days were clear and bright. Laura and Mary stood on chairs by the window and looked out across the glittering snow at the glittering trees. Snow was piled all along their bare, dark branches,

and it sparkled in the sunshine. Icicles hung from the eaves of the house to the snowbanks, great icicles as large at the top as Laura's arm. They were like glass and full of sharp lights.

Pa's breath hung in the air like smoke, when he came along the path from the barn. He breathed it out in clouds and it froze in white frost on his mustache and beard.

When he came in, stamping the snow from his boots, and caught Laura up in a bear's hug against his cold, big coat, his mustache was beaded with little drops of melting frost.

Every night he was busy, working on a large piece of board and two small pieces. He whittled them with his knife, he rubbed them with sandpaper and with the palm of his hand, until when Laura touched them they felt soft and smooth as silk.

Then with his sharp jack-knife he worked at them, cutting the edges of the large one into little peaks and towers, with a large star carved on the very tallest point. He cut little holes through the wood. He cut the holes in shapes of windows, and little stars, and crescent moons, and circles. All around them he carved tiny leaves, and flowers, and birds.

One of the little boards he shaped in a lovely curve, and around its edges he carved leaves and flowers and stars, and through it he cut crescent moons and curlicues.

Around the edges of the smallest board he carved a tiny flowering vine.

He made the tiniest shavings, cutting very slowly and carefully, making whatever he thought would be pretty.

At last he had the pieces finished and one night he fitted them together. When this was done, the large piece was a beautifully carved back for a smooth little shelf across its middle. The large star was at the very top of it. The curved piece supported the shelf underneath, and it was carved beautifully, too. And the little vine ran around the edge of the shelf.

Pa had made this bracket for a Christmas present for Ma. He hung it carefully against the log wall between the windows, and Ma stood her little china woman on the shelf.

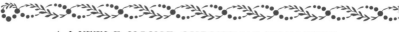

The little china woman had a china bonnet on her head, and china curls hung against her china neck. Her china dress was laced across in front, and she wore a pale pink china apron and little gilt china shoes. She was beautiful, standing on the shelf with flowers and leaves and birds and moons carved all around her, and the large star at the very top.

Ma was busy all day long, cooking good things for Christmas. She baked salt-rising bread and rye'n'Injun bread, and Swedish crackers, and a huge pan of baked beans, with salt pork and molasses. She baked vinegar pies and dried-apple pies, and filled a big jar with cookies, and she let Laura and Mary lick the cake spoon.

One morning she boiled molasses and sugar together until they made a thick syrup, and Pa brought in two pans of clean, white snow from outdoors. Laura and Mary each had a pan, and Pa and Ma showed them how to pour the dark syrup in little streams onto the snow.

They made circles, and curlicues, and squiggledy things, and these hardened at once and were candy. Laura and Mary might eat one piece each,

but the rest was saved for Christmas Day.

All this was done because Aunt Eliza and Uncle Peter and the cousins, Peter and Alice and Ella, were coming to spend Christmas.

The day before Christmas they came. Laura and Mary heard the gay ringing of sleigh bells, growing louder every moment, and then the big bobsled came out of the woods and drove up to the gate. Aunt Eliza and Uncle Peter and the cousins

were in it, all covered up, under blankets and robes and buffalo skins.

They were wrapped up in so many coats and mufflers and veils and shawls that they looked like big, shapeless bundles.

When they all came in, the little house was full and running over. Black Susan ran out and hid in the barn, but Jack leaped in circles through the snow, barking as though he would never stop. Now there were cousins to play with!

As soon as Aunt Eliza had unwrapped them, Peter and Alice and Ella and Laura and Mary began to run and shout. At last Aunt Eliza told them to be quiet. Then Alice said:

"I'll tell you what let's do. Let's make pictures."

Alice said they must go outdoors to do it, and Ma thought it was too cold for Laura to play outdoors. But when she saw how disappointed Laura was, she said she might go, after all, for a little while. She put on Laura's coat and mittens and the warm cape with the hood, and wrapped a muffler around her neck, and let her go.

Laura had never had so much fun. All morning

she played outdoors in the snow with Alice and
Ella and Peter and Mary, making pictures. The
way they did it was this:

Each one by herself climbed up on a stump,
and then all at once, holding their arms out wide,
they fell off the stumps into the soft, deep snow.
They fell flat on their faces. Then they tried to get

up without spoiling the marks they made when they fell. If they did it well, there in the snow were five holes, shaped almost exactly like four little girls and a boy, arms and legs and all. They called these their pictures.

They played so hard all day that when night came they were too excited to sleep. But they must sleep, or Santa Claus would not come. So they hung their stockings by the fireplace, and said their prayers, and went to bed—Alice and Ella and Mary and Laura all in one big bed on the floor.

Peter had the trundle bed. Aunt Eliza and Uncle Peter were going to sleep in the big bed, and another bed was made on the attic floor for Pa and Ma. The buffalo robes and all the blankets

had been brought in from Uncle Peter's sled, so there were enough covers for everybody.

Pa and Ma and Aunt Eliza and Uncle Peter sat by the fire, talking. And just as Laura was drifting off to sleep, she heard Uncle Peter say:

"Eliza had a narrow squeak the other day, when I was away at Lake City. You know Prince, that big dog of mine?"

Laura was wide awake at once. She always liked to hear about dogs. She lay still as a mouse, and looked at the fire-light flickering on the log walls, and listened to Uncle Peter.

"Well," Uncle Peter said, "early in the morning Eliza started to the spring to get a pail of water, and Prince was following her. She got to the edge of the ravine, where the path goes down to the spring, and all of a sudden Prince set his teeth in the back of her skirt and pulled.

"You know what a big dog he is. Eliza scolded him, but he wouldn't let go, and he's so big and strong she couldn't get away from him. He kept backing and pulling, till he tore a piece out of her skirt."

"It was my blue print," Aunt Eliza said to Ma.

"Dear me!" Ma said.

"He tore a big piece right out of the back of it," Aunt Eliza said. "I was so mad I could have whipped him for it. But he growled at me."

"Prince growled at you?" Pa said.

"Yes," said Aunt Eliza.

"So then she started on again toward the spring," Uncle Peter went on. "But Prince jumped into the path ahead of her and snarled at her. He paid no attention to her talking and scolding. He just kept on showing his teeth and snarling, and when she tried to get past him he kept in front of her and snapped at her. That scared her."

"I should think it would!" Ma said.

"He was so savage, I thought he was going to bite me," said Aunt Eliza. "I believe he would have."

"I never heard of such a thing!" said Ma. "What on earth did you do?"

 "I turned right around and ran into the house where the children were,

and slammed the door," Aunt Eliza answered.

"Of course Prince was savage with strangers," said Uncle Peter. "But he was always so kind to Eliza and the children I felt perfectly safe to leave them with him. Eliza couldn't understand it at all.

"After she got into the house he kept pacing around it and growling. Every time she started to open the door he jumped at her and snarled."

"Had he gone mad?" said Ma.

"That's what I thought," Aunt Eliza said. "I didn't know what to do. There I was, shut up in the house with the children, and not daring to go out. And we didn't have any water. I couldn't even get any snow to melt. Every time I opened the door so much as a crack, Prince acted like he would tear me to pieces."

"How long did this go on?" Pa asked.

"All day, till late in the afternoon," Aunt Eliza said. "Peter had taken the gun, or I would have shot him."

"Along late in the afternoon," Uncle Peter said, "he got quiet, and lay down in front of the door. Eliza thought he was asleep, and she made

up her mind to try to slip past him and get to the spring for some water.

"So she opened the door very quietly, but of course he woke up right away. When he saw she had the water pail in her hand, he got up and walked ahead of her to the spring, just the same as usual. And there, all around the spring in the snow, were the fresh tracks of a panther."

"The tracks were as big as my hand," said Aunt Eliza.

"Yes," Uncle Peter said, "he was a big fellow. His tracks were the biggest I ever saw. He would have got Eliza sure, if Prince had let her go to the spring in the morning. I saw the tracks. He had been lying up in that big oak over the spring, waiting for some animal to come there for water. Undoubtedly he would have dropped down on her.

"Night was coming on, when she saw the tracks, and she didn't waste any time getting back to the house with her pail of water. Prince followed close behind her, looking back into the ravine now and then."

"I took him into the house with me," Aunt

Eliza said, "and we all stayed inside, till Peter came home."

"Did you get him?" Pa asked Uncle Peter.

"No," Uncle Peter said. "I took my gun and hunted all round the place, but I couldn't find him. I saw some more of his tracks. He'd gone on north, farther into the Big Woods."

Alice and Ella and Mary were all wide awake now, and Laura put her head under the covers and whispered to Alice, "My! weren't you scared?"

Alice whispered back that she was scared, but Ella was scareder. And Ella whispered that she wasn't, either, any such thing.

"Well, anyway, you made more fuss about being thirsty," Alice whispered.

They lay there whispering about it till Ma said: "Charles, those children never will get to sleep unless you play for them." So Pa got his fiddle.

The room was still and warm and full of fire-light. Ma's shadow, and Aunt Eliza's and Uncle Peter's were big and quivering on the walls in the flickering fire-light, and Pa's fiddle sang merrily to itself.

It sang "Money Musk," and "The Red Heifer," "The Devil's Dream," and "Arkansas Traveler." And Laura went to sleep while Pa and the fiddle were both softly singing:

> *"My darling Nelly Gray, they have taken*
> *you away,*
> *And I'll never see my darling any more. . . ."*

In the morning they all woke up almost at the same moment. They looked at their stockings, and something was in them. Santa Claus had been there. Alice and Ella and Laura in their red flannel nightgowns, and Peter in his red flannel nightshirt, all ran shouting to see what he had brought.

In each stocking there was a pair of bright red mittens, and there was a long, flat stick of red-and-white-striped peppermint candy, all beautifully notched along each side.

They were all so happy they could hardly speak at first. They just looked with shining eyes at those lovely Christmas presents. But Laura was happiest of all. Laura had a rag doll.

She was a beautiful doll. She had a face of white cloth with black button eyes. A black pencil had

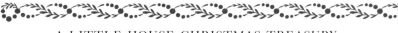
made her eyebrows, and her cheeks and her mouth were red with the ink made from pokeberries. Her hair was black yarn that had been knit and raveled, so that it was curly.

She had little red flannel stockings and little black cloth gaiters for shoes, and her dress was pretty pink and blue calico.

She was so beautiful that Laura could not say a word. She just held her tight and forgot everything else. She did not know that everyone was looking at her, till Aunt Eliza said:

"Did you ever see such big eyes!"

The other girls were not jealous because Laura had mittens, and candy, *and* a doll, because Laura was the littlest girl, except Baby Carrie and Aunt Eliza's little baby, Dolly Varden. The babies were too small for dolls. They were so small they did not even know about Santa Claus. They just put their fingers in their mouths and wriggled because of all the excitement.

Laura sat down on the edge of the bed and held her doll. She loved her red mittens and she loved the candy, but she loved her doll best of all.

She named her Charlotte.

Then they all looked at each other's mittens, and tried on their own, and Peter bit a large piece out of his stick of candy, but Alice and Ella and Mary and Laura licked theirs, to make it last longer.

"Well, well!" Uncle Peter said. "Isn't there even one stocking with nothing but a switch in it? My, my, have you all been such good children?"

But they didn't believe that Santa Claus could, really, have given any of them nothing but a switch. That happened to some children, but it couldn't happen to them. It was so hard to be good all the time, every day, for a whole year.

"You mustn't tease the children, Peter," Aunt Eliza said.

Ma said, "Laura, aren't you going to let the other girls hold your doll?" She meant, "Little girls must not be so selfish."

So Laura let Mary take the beautiful doll, and then Alice held her a minute, and then Ella. They smoothed the pretty dress and admired the red flannel stockings and the gaiters, and the curly woolen hair. But Laura was glad when at last Charlotte was safe in her arms again.

Pa and Uncle Peter had each a pair of new, warm mittens, knit in little squares of red and white. Ma and Aunt Eliza had made them.

Aunt Eliza had brought Ma a large red apple stuck full of cloves. How good it smelled! And it would not spoil, for so many cloves would keep it sound and sweet.

Ma gave Aunt Eliza a little needle-book she had made, with bits of silk for covers and soft white flannel leaves into which to stick the needles. The flannel would keep the needles from rusting.

They all admired Ma's beautiful bracket, and Aunt Eliza said that Uncle Peter had made one for her—of course, with different carving.

Santa Claus had not given them anything at all. Santa Claus did not give grown people presents, but that was not because they had not been good. Pa and Ma were good. It was because they were grown up, and grown people must give each other presents.

Then all the presents must be laid away for a little while. Peter went out with Pa and Uncle Peter

to do the chores, and Alice and Ella helped Aunt Eliza make the beds, and Laura and Mary set the table, while Ma got breakfast.

For breakfast there were pancakes, and Ma made a pancake man for each one of the children. Ma called each one in turn to bring her plate, and each could stand by the stove and watch, while with the spoonful of batter Ma put on the arms and the legs and the head. It was exciting to watch her turn the whole little man over, quickly and carefully, on a hot griddle. When it was done, she put it smoking hot on the plate.

Peter ate the head off his man, right away. But Alice and Ella and Mary and Laura ate theirs slowly in little bits, first the arms and legs and then the middle, saving the head for the last.

Today the weather was so cold that they could not play outdoors, but there were the new mittens to admire, and the candy to lick. And they all sat on the floor together and looked at the pictures in the Bible, and the pictures of all kinds of animals and birds in Pa's big green book. Laura kept Charlotte in her arms the whole time.

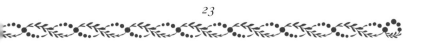

Then there was the Christmas dinner. Alice and Ella and Peter and Mary and Laura did not say a word at table, for they knew that children should be seen and not heard. But they did not need to ask for second helpings. Ma and Aunt Eliza kept their plates full and let them eat all the good things they could hold.

"Christmas comes but once a year," said Aunt Eliza.

Dinner was early, because Aunt Eliza, Uncle Peter and the cousins had such a long way to go.

"Best the horses can do," Uncle Peter said, "we'll hardly make it home before dark."

So as soon as they had eaten dinner, Uncle Peter and Pa went to put the horses to the sled, while Ma and Aunt Eliza wrapped up the cousins.

They pulled heavy woolen stockings over the woolen stockings and the shoes they were already wearing. They put on mittens and coats and warm hoods and shawls, and wrapped mufflers around their necks and thick woolen veils over their faces. Ma slipped piping hot baked potatoes into their pockets to keep their fingers warm, and Aunt

Eliza's flatirons were hot on the stove, ready to put at their feet in the sled. The blankets and the quilts and the buffalo robes were warmed, too.

So they all got into the big bobsled, cosy and warm, and Pa tucked the last robe well in around them.

"Good-by! Good-by!" they called, and off they went, the horses trotting gaily and the sleigh bells ringing.

In just a little while the merry sound of the bells was gone, and Christmas was over. But what a happy Christmas it had been!

*L*aura is six years old now, and she and her family have traveled in their covered wagon to a new little house all the way out on the wide-open prairie in Indian Territory. Cold rain has been falling for days and days, and Laura and Mary are worried: Everyone knows that Santa Claus and his reindeer need snow to travel by sleigh. But Christmas Eve is here, and no snow has fallen.

Will Santa make it to the little house on the prairie in time for Christmas morning?

Christmas
on the
Prairie

Mr. Edwards Meets
Santa Claus

THE DAYS WERE SHORT AND COLD, THE WIND whistled sharply, but there was no snow. Cold rains were falling. Day after day the rain fell, pattering on the roof and pouring from the eaves.

Mary and Laura stayed close by the fire, sewing their nine-patch quilt blocks, or cutting paper dolls from scraps of wrapping-paper, and hearing the wet sound of the rain. Every night was so cold that they expected to see snow next morning, but in the morning they saw only sad, wet grass.

They pressed their noses against the squares of glass in the windows that Pa had made, and they

were glad they could see out. But they wished they could see snow.

Laura was anxious because Christmas was near, and Santa Claus and his reindeer could not travel without snow. Mary was afraid that, even if it snowed, Santa Claus could not find them, so far away in Indian Territory. When they asked Ma about this, she said she didn't know.

"What day is it?" they asked her, anxiously. "How many more days till Christmas?" And they counted off the days on their fingers, till there was only one more day left.

Rain was still falling that morning. There was not one crack in the gray sky. They felt almost sure there would be no Christmas. Still, they kept hoping.

Just before noon the light changed. The clouds broke and drifted apart, shining white in a clear blue sky. The sun shone, birds sang, and thousands of drops of water sparkled on the grasses. But when Ma opened the door to let in the fresh, cold air, they heard the creek roaring.

They had not thought about the creek. Now they knew they would have no Christmas, because Santa Claus could not cross that roaring creek.

Pa came in, bringing a big fat turkey. If it weighed less than twenty pounds, he said, he'd eat it, feathers and all. He asked Laura, "How's that for a Christmas dinner? Think you can manage one of those drumsticks?"

She said, yes, she could. But she was sober.

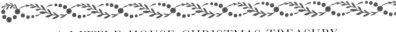
Then Mary asked him if the creek was going down, and he said it was still rising.

Ma said it was too bad. She hated to think of Mr. Edwards eating his bachelor cooking all alone on Christmas day. Mr. Edwards had been asked to eat Christmas dinner with them, but Pa shook his head and said a man would risk his neck, trying to cross that creek now.

"No," he said. "That current's too strong. We'll just have to make up our minds that Edwards won't be here tomorrow."

Of course that meant that Santa Claus could not come, either.

Laura and Mary tried not to mind too much. They watched Ma dress the wild turkey, and it was a very fat turkey. They were lucky little girls, to have a good house to live in, and a warm fire to sit by, and such a turkey for their Christmas dinner. Ma said so, and it was true. Ma said it was too bad that Santa Claus couldn't come this year, but they were such good girls that he hadn't forgotten them; he would surely come next year.

Still, they were not happy.

After supper that night they washed their hands and faces, buttoned their red-flannel nightgowns, tied their night-cap strings, and soberly said their prayers. They lay down in bed and pulled the covers up. It did not seem at all like Christmas time.

Pa and Ma sat silent by the fire. After a while Ma asked why Pa didn't play the fiddle, and he said, "I don't seem to have the heart to, Caroline."

After a longer while, Ma suddenly stood up.

"I'm going to hang up your stockings, girls," she said. "Maybe something will happen."

Laura's heart jumped. But then she thought again of the creek and she knew nothing could happen.

Ma took one of Mary's clean stockings and one of Laura's, and she hung them from the mantel-shelf, on either side of the fireplace. Laura and Mary watched her over the edge of their bed-covers.

"Now go to sleep," Ma said, kissing them good night. "Morning will come quicker if you're asleep."

She sat down again by the fire and Laura almost

went to sleep. She woke up a little when she heard Pa say, "You've only made it worse, Caroline." And she thought she heard Ma say: "No, Charles. There's the white sugar." But perhaps she was dreaming.

Then she heard Jack growl savagely. The door-latch rattled and someone said, "Ingalls! Ingalls!" Pa was stirring up the fire, and when he opened the door Laura saw that it was morning. The outdoors was gray.

"Great fishhooks, Edwards! Come in, man! What's happened?" Pa exclaimed.

Laura saw the stockings limply dangling, and she scrooged her shut eyes into the pillow. She heard Pa piling wood on the fire, and she heard Mr. Edwards say he had carried his clothes on his head when he swam the creek. His teeth rattled and his voice shivered. He would be all right, he said, as soon as he got warm.

"It was too big a risk, Edwards," Pa said. "We're glad you're here, but that was too big a risk for a Christmas dinner."

"Your little ones had to have a Christmas," Mr.

Edwards replied. "No creek could stop me, after I fetched them their gifts from Independence."

Laura sat straight up in bed. "Did you see Santa Claus?" she shouted.

"I sure did," Mr. Edwards said.

"Where? When? What did he look like? What did he say? Did he really give you something for us?" Mary and Laura cried.

"Wait, wait a minute!" Mr. Edwards laughed. And Ma said she would put the presents in the stockings, as Santa Claus intended. She said they mustn't look.

Mr. Edwards came and sat on the floor by their bed, and he answered every question they asked him. They honestly tried not to look at Ma, and they didn't quite see what she was doing.

When he saw the creek rising, Mr. Edwards said, he had known that Santa Claus could not get across it. ("But you crossed it," Laura said. "Yes,"  Mr. Edwards replied, "but Santa Claus is too old and fat. He couldn't make it, where a long, lean razor-back like me could do so.") And Mr. Edwards reasoned that if Santa Claus couldn't cross the creek, likely he would come no farther south than Independence. Why should he come forty miles across the prairie, only to be turned back? Of course he wouldn't do that!

So Mr. Edwards had walked to Independence. ("In the rain?" Mary asked. Mr. Edwards said he wore his rubber coat.) And there, coming down the street in Independence, he had met Santa Claus. ("In the daytime?" Laura asked. She hadn't thought that anyone could see Santa Claus in the daytime. No, Mr. Edwards said; it was night, but light shone out across the street from the saloons.)

Well, the first thing Santa Claus said was, "Hello, Edwards!" ("Did he know you?" Mary asked, and Laura asked, "How did you know he was really Santa Claus?" Mr. Edwards said that Santa Claus knew everybody. And he had recognized Santa at once by his whiskers. Santa Claus had the longest, thickest, whitest set of whiskers west of the Mississippi.)

So Santa Claus said, "Hello, Edwards! Last time I saw you you were sleeping on a corn-shuck bed in Tennessee." And Mr. Edwards well remembered the little pair of red-yarn mittens that Santa Claus had left for him that time.

Then Santa Claus said: "I understand you're living now down along the Verdigris River. Have you ever met up, down yonder, with two little young girls named Mary and Laura?"

"I surely am acquainted with them," Mr. Edwards replied.

"It rests heavy on my mind," said Santa Claus. "They are both of them sweet, pretty, good little young things, and I know they are expecting me. I surely do hate to disappoint two good little

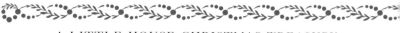

girls like them. Yet with the water up the way it is, I can't ever make it across that creek. I can figure no way whatsoever to get to their cabin this year. Edwards," Santa Claus said. "Would you do me the favor to fetch them their gifts this one time?"

"I'll do that, and with pleasure," Mr. Edwards told him.

Then Santa Claus and Mr. Edwards stepped across the street to the hitching-posts where the pack-mule was tied. ("Didn't he have his reindeer?" Laura asked. "You know he couldn't," Mary said. "There isn't any snow." Exactly, said Mr. Edwards. Santa Claus traveled with a pack-mule in the southwest.)

And Santa Claus uncinched the pack and looked through it, and he took out the presents for Mary and Laura.

"Oh, what are they?" Laura cried; but Mary asked, "Then what did he do?"

Then he shook hands with Mr. Edwards, and he swung up on his fine bay horse. Santa Claus rode well for a man of his weight and build. And he tucked his long, white whiskers under his bandana.

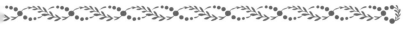

"So long, Edwards," he said, and he rode away on the Fort Dodge trail, leading his pack-mule and whistling.

Laura and Mary were silent an instant, thinking of that.

Then Ma said, "You may look now, girls."

Something was shining bright in the top of Laura's stocking. She squealed and jumped out of bed. So did Mary, but Laura beat her to the

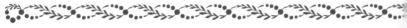
fireplace. And the shining thing was a glittering new tin cup.

Mary had one exactly like it.

These new tin cups were their very own. Now they each had a cup to drink out of. Laura jumped up and down and shouted and laughed, but Mary stood still and looked with shining eyes at her own tin cup.

Then they plunged their hands into the stockings again. And they pulled out two long, long sticks of candy. It was peppermint candy, striped red and white. They looked and looked at the beautiful candy, and Laura licked her stick, just one lick. But Mary was not so greedy. She didn't take even one lick of her stick.

Those stockings weren't empty yet. Mary and Laura pulled out two small packages. They unwrapped them, and each found a little heart-shaped cake. Over their delicate brown tops was sprinkled white sugar. The sparkling grains lay like tiny drifts of snow.

The cakes were too pretty to eat. Mary and Laura just looked at them. But at last Laura turned

hers over, and she nibbled a tiny nibble from underneath, where it wouldn't show. And the inside of the little cake was white!

It had been made of pure white flour, and sweetened with white sugar.

Laura and Mary never would have looked in their stockings again. The cups and the cakes and the candy were almost too much. They were too happy to speak. But Ma asked if they were sure the stockings were empty.

Then they put their hands down inside them, to make sure.

And in the very toe of each stocking was a shining bright, new penny!

They had never even thought of such a thing as having a penny. Think of having a whole penny for your very own. Think of having a cup and a cake and a stick of candy *and* a penny.

There never had been such a Christmas.

Now of course, right away, Laura and Mary should have thanked Mr. Edwards for bringing those lovely presents all the way from Independence. But they had forgotten all about

Mr. Edwards. They had even forgotten Santa Claus. In a minute they would have remembered, but before they did, Ma said, gently, "Aren't you going to thank Mr. Edwards?"

"Oh, thank you, Mr. Edwards! Thank you!" they said, and they meant it with all their hearts. Pa shook Mr. Edwards' hand, too, and shook it again. Pa and Ma and Mr. Edwards acted as if they were almost crying, Laura didn't know why. So she gazed again at her beautiful presents.

She looked up again when Ma gasped. And Mr. Edwards was taking sweet potatoes out of his pockets. He said they had helped to balance the package on his head when he swam across the creek. He thought Pa and Ma might like them, with the Christmas turkey.

There were nine sweet potatoes. Mr. Edwards had brought them all the way from town, too. It was just too much. Pa said so. "It's too much, Edwards," he said. They never could thank him enough.

Mary and Laura were too excited to eat breakfast. They drank the milk from their shining new

cups. but they could not swallow the rabbit stew and the cornmeal mush.

"Don't make them, Charles," Ma said. "It will soon be dinner-time."

For Christmas dinner there was the tender, juicy, roasted turkey. There were the sweet potatoes, baked in the ashes and carefully wiped so that you could eat the good skins, too. There was a loaf of salt-rising bread made from the last of the white flour.

And after all that there were stewed dried blackberries and little cakes. But these little cakes were made with brown sugar and they did not have white sugar sprinkled over their tops.

Then Pa and Ma and Mr. Edwards sat by the fire and talked about Christmas times back in Tennessee and up north in the Big Woods. But Mary and Laura looked at their beautiful cakes and played with their pennies and drank their water out of their new cups. And little by little they licked and sucked their sticks of candy, till each stick was sharp-pointed on one end.

That was a happy Christmas.

The Ingalls family has packed up the covered wagon once again and moved from the little house on the prairie to the banks of Plum Creek in Minnesota. Eight-year-old Laura is worried because there is no fireplace or chimney in their new little sod house, but Ma assures her that Santa Claus will be able to find them anyway. Laura and Mary know just what they want for Christmas this year—until Ma helps them understand the special meaning of Christmas wishes.

Christmas
on
Plum Creek

The Christmas Horses

GRASSHOPPER WEATHER WAS STRANGE weather. Even at Thanksgiving, there was no snow.

The door of the dugout was wide open while they ate Thanksgiving dinner. Laura could see across the bare willow-tops, far over the prairie to the place where the sun would go down. There was not one speck of snow. The prairie was like soft yellow fur. The line where it met the sky was not sharp now; it was smudged and blurry.

"Grasshopper weather," Laura thought to herself. She thought of grasshoppers' long, folded

wings and their high-jointed hind legs. Their feet were thin and scratchy. Their heads were hard, with large eyes on the corners, and their jaws were tiny and nibbling.

If you caught a grasshopper and held him, and gently poked a green blade of grass into his jaws, they nibbled it fast. They swiftly nibbled in the whole grass blade, till the tip of it went into them and was gone.

Thanksgiving dinner was good. Pa had shot a wild goose for it. Ma had to stew the goose because there was no fireplace, and no oven in the little stove. But she made dumplings in the gravy. There were corn dodgers and mashed potatoes. There were butter, and milk, and stewed dried plums. And three grains of parched corn lay beside each tin plate.

At the first Thanksgiving dinner the poor Pilgrims had nothing to eat but three parched grains of corn. Then the Indians came and brought them turkeys, so the Pilgrims were thankful.

Now, after they had eaten their good, big Thanksgiving dinner, Laura and Mary could eat

their grains of corn and remember the Pilgrims. Parched corn was good. It crackled and crunched, and its taste was sweet and brown.

Then Thanksgiving was past and it was time to think of Christmas. Still there was no snow and no rain. The sky was gray, the prairie was dull, and the winds were cold. But the cold winds blew over the top of the dugout.

"A dugout is snug and cosy," said Ma. "But I do feel like an animal penned up for the winter."

"Never mind, Caroline," Pa said. "We'll have a good house next year." His eyes shone and his voice was like singing. "And good horses, and a buggy to boot! I'll take you riding, dressed up in silks! Think, Caroline—this level, rich land, not a stone or stump to contend with, and only three miles from a railroad! We can sell every grain of wheat we raise!"

Then he ran his fingers through his hair and said, "I do wish I had a team of horses."

"Now, Charles," said Ma. "Here we are, all healthy and safe and snug, with food for the winter. Let's be thankful for what we have."

"I am," Pa said. "But Pete and Bright are too slow for harrowing and harvesting. I've broken up that big field with them, but I can't put it all in wheat, without horses."

Then Laura had a chance to speak without interrupting. She said, "There isn't any fireplace."

"Whatever are you talking about?" Ma asked her.

"Santa Claus," Laura answered.

"Eat your supper, Laura, and let's not cross bridges till we come to them," said Ma.

Laura and Mary knew that Santa Claus could not come down a chimney where there was no chimney. One day Mary asked Ma how Santa Claus would come. Ma did not answer. Instead, she asked, "What do you girls want for Christmas?"

She was ironing. One end of the ironing-board was on the table and the other on the bedstead. Pa had made the bedstead that high, on purpose. Carrie was playing on the bed and Laura and Mary sat at the table. Mary was sorting quilt blocks and Laura was making a little apron for the rag doll, Charlotte. The wind howled overhead and whined in the stovepipe, but there was no snow yet.

Laura said, "I want candy."

"So do I," said Mary, and Carrie cried, "Tandy?"

"And a new winter dress, and a coat, and a hood," said Mary.

"So do I," said Laura. "And a dress for Charlotte, and—"

Ma lifted the iron from the stove and held it out to them. They could test the iron. They licked their fingers and touched them, quicker than quick, to the smooth hot bottom. If it crackled, the iron was hot enough.

"Thank you, Mary and Laura," Ma said. She began carefully ironing around and over the patches on Pa's shirt. "Do you know what Pa wants for Christmas?"

They did not know.

"Horses," Ma said. "Would you girls like horses?"

Laura and Mary looked at each other.

"I only thought," Ma went on, "if we all wished for horses, and nothing but horses, then maybe—"

Laura felt queer. Horses were everyday; they

were not Christmas. If Pa got horses, he would trade for them. Laura could not think of Santa Claus and horses at the same time.

"Ma!" she cried. "There IS a Santa Claus, isn't there?"

"Of course there's a Santa Claus," said Ma. She set the iron on the stove to heat again.

"The older you are, the more you know about Santa Claus," she said. "You are so big now, you know he can't be just one man, don't you? You know he is everywhere on Christmas Eve. He is in the Big Woods, and in Indian Territory, and far away in New York State, and here. He comes down all the chimneys at the same time. You know that, don't you?"

"Yes, Ma," said Mary and Laura.

"Well," said Ma. "Then you see—"

"I guess he is like angels," Mary said, slowly. And Laura could see that, just as well as Mary could.

Then Ma told them something else about Santa Claus. He was everywhere, and besides that, he was all the time.

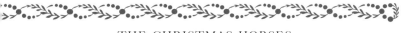
Whenever anyone was unselfish, that was Santa Claus.

Christmas Eve was the time when everybody was unselfish. On that one night, Santa Claus was everywhere, because everybody, all together, stopped being selfish and wanted other people to be happy. And in the morning you saw what that had done.

"If everybody wanted everybody else to be happy, all the time, then would it be Christmas all the time?" Laura asked, and Ma said, "Yes, Laura."

Laura thought about that. So did Mary. They thought, and they looked at each other, and they knew what Ma wanted them to do. She wanted them to wish for nothing but horses for Pa. They looked at each other again and they looked away quickly and they did not say anything. Even Mary, who was always so good, did not say a word.

That night after supper Pa drew Laura and Mary close to him in the crook of his arms. Laura looked up at his face, and then she snuggled against him and said, "Pa."

"What is it, little half-pint of sweet

cider?" Pa asked, and Laura said:

"Pa, I want Santa Claus—to bring—"

"What?" Pa asked.

"Horses," said Laura. "If you will let me ride them sometimes."

"So do I!" said Mary. But Laura had said it first.

Pa was surprised. His eyes shone soft and bright at them. "Would you girls really like horses?" he asked them.

"Oh yes, Pa!" they said.

"In that case," said Pa, smiling, "I have an idea that Santa Claus will bring us all a fine team of horses."

That settled it. They would not have any Christmas, only horses. Laura and Mary soberly undressed and soberly buttoned up their nightgowns and tied their nightcap strings. They knelt down together and said,

"Now I lay me down to sleep,
I pray the Lord my soul to keep.
If I should die before I wake
I pray the Lord my soul to take,

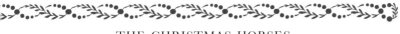
and please bless Pa and Ma and Carrie and every-
body and make me a good girl for ever'n'ever.
Amen."

Quickly Laura added, in her own head, "And
please make me only glad about the Christmas
horses, for ever'n'ever amen again."

She climbed into bed and almost right away she
was glad. She thought of horses sleek and shining,
of how their manes and tails blew in the wind, how
they picked up their swift feet and sniffed the air
with velvety noses and looked at everything with
bright, soft eyes. And Pa would let her ride them.

Pa had tuned his fiddle and now he set it
against his shoulder. Overhead the wind went wail-
ing lonely in the cold dark. But in the dugout
everything was snug and cosy.

Bits of fire-light came through the seams of the
stove and twinkled on Ma's steel knitting needles
and tried to catch Pa's elbow. In the shadows the
bow was dancing, on the floor Pa's toe was tapping,
and the merry music hid the lonely crying of the
wind.

A Merry Christmas

NEXT MORNING, SNOW WAS IN THE AIR. Hard bits of snow were leaping and whirling in the howling wind.

Laura could not go out to play. In the stable, Spot and Pete and Bright stood all day long, eating the hay and straw. In the dugout, Pa mended his boots while Ma read to him again the story called *Millbank*. Mary sewed and Laura played with Charlotte. She could let Carrie hold Charlotte, but Carrie was too little to play with paper dolls; she might tear one.

That afternoon, when Carrie was asleep, Ma

beckoned Mary and Laura. Her face was shining with a secret. They put their heads close to hers, and she told them. They could make a button-string for Carrie's Christmas!

They climbed onto their bed and turned their backs to Carrie and spread their laps wide. Ma brought them her button-box.

The box was almost full. Ma had saved buttons since she was smaller than Laura, and she had buttons her mother had saved when her mother was a little girl. There were blue buttons and red buttons, silvery and goldy buttons, curved-in buttons with tiny raised castles and bridges and trees on them, and twinkling jet buttons, painted china buttons, striped buttons, buttons like juicy blackberries, and even one tiny dog-head button. Laura squealed when she saw it.

"Sh!" Ma shushed her. But Carrie did not wake up.

Ma gave them all those buttons to make a button string for Carrie.

After that, Laura did not mind staying in the dugout. When she saw the outdoors, the wind was

driving snowdrifts across the bare frozen land. The creek was ice and the willow-tops rattled. In the dugout she and Mary had their secret.

They played gently with Carrie and gave her everything she wanted. They cuddled her and sang to her and got her to sleep whenever they could. Then they worked on the button-string.

Mary had one end of the string and Laura had the other. They picked out the buttons they wanted and strung them on the string. They held the string out and looked at it, and took off some buttons and put on others. Sometimes they took every button off, and started again. They were going to make the most beautiful button-string in the world.

One day Ma told them that this was the day before Christmas. They must finish the button-string that day.

They could not get Carrie to sleep. She ran and shouted, climbed on benches and jumped off, and skipped and sang. She did not get tired. Mary told her to sit still like a little lady, but she wouldn't. Laura let her hold Charlotte, and she jounced Charlotte up and down and flung her against the wall.

Finally Ma cuddled her and sang. Laura and Mary were perfectly still. Lower and lower Ma sang, and Carrie's eyes blinked till they shut. When softly Ma stopped singing, Carrie's eyes popped open and she shouted, "More, Ma! More!"

But at last she fell asleep. Then quickly, quickly, Laura and Mary finished the button-string. Ma tied the ends together for them. It was done; they could not change one button more. It was a beautiful button-string.

That evening after supper, when Carrie was sound asleep, Ma hung her clean little pair of stockings from the table edge. Laura and Mary, in their nightgowns, slid the button-string into one stocking.

Then that was all. Mary and Laura were going

to bed when Pa asked them, "Aren't you girls going to hang your stockings?"

"But I thought," Laura said, "I thought Santa Claus was going to bring us horses."

"Maybe he will," said Pa. "But little girls always hang up their stockings on Christmas Eve, don't they?"

Laura did not know what to think. Neither did Mary. Ma took two clean stockings out of the clothes-box, and Pa helped hang them beside Carrie's. Laura and Mary said their prayers and went to sleep, wondering.

In the morning Laura heard the fire crackling. She opened one eye the least bit, and saw lamplight, and a bulge in her Christmas stocking.

She yelled and jumped out of bed. Mary came running, too, and Carrie woke up. In Laura's stocking, and in Mary's stocking, there were little paper packages, just alike. In the packages was candy.

Laura had six pieces, and Mary had six. They had never seen such beautiful candy. It was too beautiful to eat. Some pieces were like ribbons,

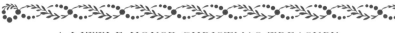

bent in waves. Some were short bits of round stick candy, and on their flat ends were colored flowers that went all the way through. Some were perfectly round and striped.

In one of Carrie's stockings were four pieces of that beautiful candy. In the other was the button-string. Carrie's eyes and her mouth were perfectly round when she saw it. Then she squealed, and grabbed it and squealed again. She sat on Pa's knee, looking at her candy and her button-string and wriggling and laughing with joy.

Then it was time for Pa to do the chores. He said, "Do you suppose there is anything for us in the stable?" And Ma said, "Dress as fast as you can, girls, and you can go to the stable and see what Pa finds."

It was winter, so they had to put on stockings and shoes. But Ma helped them button up the shoes and she pinned their shawls under their chins. They ran out into the cold.

Everything was gray, except a long red streak in the eastern sky. Its red light shone on the patches of gray-white snow. Snow was caught in the dead

grass on the walls and roof of the stable and it was red. Pa stood waiting in the stable door. He laughed when he saw Laura and Mary, and he stepped outside to let them go in.

There, standing in Pete's and Bright's places, were two horses.

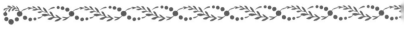

They were larger than Pet and Patty, and they were a soft, red-brown color, shining like silk. Their manes and tails were black. Their eyes were bright and gentle. They put their velvety noses down to Laura and nibbled softly at her hand and breathed warm on it.

"Well, flutterbudget!" said Pa. "And Mary. How do you girls like your Christmas?"

"Very much, Pa," said Mary, but Laura could only say, "Oh, Pa!"

Pa's eyes shone deep and he asked, "Who wants to ride the Christmas horses to water?"

Laura could hardly wait while he lifted Mary up and showed her how to hold on to the mane, and told her not to be afraid. Then Pa's strong hands swung Laura up. She sat on the horse's big, gentle back and felt its aliveness carrying her.

All outdoors was glittering now with sunshine on snow and frost. Pa went ahead, leading the horses and carrying his ax to break the ice in the creek so they could drink. The horses lifted their heads and took deep breaths and whooshed the cold out of their noses. Their velvety ears pricked forward, then back and forward again.

Laura held to her horse's mane and clapped her shoes together and laughed. Pa and the horses and Mary and Laura were all happy in the gay, cold Christmas morning.

It's nearly Christmastime again on the banks of Plum Creek, and Laura and Mary keep warm inside their cozy little house. One day Ma surprises them with the news that they will all go to town that night. But why? They've never gone to town after dark! As they ride in the back of the wagon, dressed up in their finest clothes, Laura and Mary whisper and wonder about what awaits them. The night sky is dark, and the shops are closed up, but the church is full of light. And inside, it holds a Christmas surprise unlike anything Laura's ever seen before.

Surprise

THAT WAS ANOTHER MILD WINTER WITHOUT much snow. It was still grasshopper weather. But chill winds blew, the sky was gray, and the best place for little girls was in the cosy house.

Pa was gone outdoors all day. He hauled logs and chopped them into wood for the stove. He followed frozen Plum Creek far upstream where nobody lived, and set traps along the banks for muskrat and otter and mink.

Every morning Laura and Mary studied their books and worked sums on the slate. Every afternoon Ma heard their lessons. She said they were

good little scholars, and she was sure that when they went to school again they would find they had kept up with their classes.

Every Sunday they went to Sunday school. Laura saw Nellie Oleson showing off her fur cape. She remembered what Nellie had said about Pa, and she burned hot inside. She knew that hot feeling was wicked. She knew she must forgive Nellie, or she would never be an angel. She thought hard about the pictures of beautiful angels in the big paper-covered Bible at home. But they wore long white nightgowns. Not one of them wore a fur cape.

One happy Sunday was the Sunday when the Reverend Alden came from eastern Minnesota to preach in this western church. He preached for a long time, while Laura looked at his soft blue eyes

and watched his beard wagging. She hoped he would speak to her after church. And he did.

"Here are my little country girls, Mary and Laura!" he said. He remembered their names.

Laura was wearing her new dress that day. The skirt was long enough, and the sleeves were long, too. They made her coat sleeves look shorter than ever, but the red braid on the cuffs was pretty.

"What a pretty new dress, Laura!" the Reverend Alden said.

Laura almost forgave Nellie Oleson that day. Then came Sundays when the Reverend Alden stayed at his own far church and in Sunday school Nellie Oleson turned up her nose at Laura and flounced her shoulders under the fur cape. Hot wickedness boiled up in Laura again.

One afternoon Ma said there would be no lessons, because they must all get ready to go to town that night. Laura and Mary were astonished.

"But we never go to town at night!" Mary said.

"There must always be a first time," said Ma.

"But why must there be, Ma?" Laura asked.

"Why are we going to town at night?"

"It's a surprise," said Ma. "Now, no more questions. We must all take baths, and be our very nicest."

In the middle of the week, Ma brought in the washtub and heated water for Mary's bath. Then again for Laura's bath, and again for Carrie's. There had never been such scrubbing and scampering, such a changing to fresh drawers and petticoats, such brushing of shoes and braiding of hair and tying on of hair ribbons. There had never been such a wondering.

Supper was early. After supper, Pa bathed in the bedroom. Laura and Mary put on their new dresses. They knew better than to ask any more questions, but they wondered and whispered together.

The wagon box was full of clean hay. Pa put Mary and Laura in it and wrapped blankets around them. He climbed to the seat beside Ma and drove away toward town.

The stars were small and frosty in the dark sky. The horses' feet clippety-clopped

and the wagon rattled over the hard ground.

Pa heard something else. "Whoa!" he said, pulling up the reins. Sam and David stopped. There was nothing but vast, dark coldness and stillness pricked by the stars. Then the stillness blossomed into the loveliest sound.

Two clear notes sounded, and sounded again and again.

No one moved. Only Sam and David tinkled their bits together and breathed. Those two notes went on, full and loud, soft and low. They seemed to be the stars singing.

Too soon Ma murmured, "We'd better be getting on, Charles," and the wagon rattled on. Still through its rattling Laura could hear those swaying notes.

"Oh, Pa, what is it?" she asked, and Pa said, "It's the new churchbell, Laura."

It was for this that Pa had worn his old patched boots.

The town seemed asleep. The stores were dark as Pa drove past them. Then Laura exclaimed,

"Oh, look at the church! How pretty the church is!"

The church was full of light. Light spilled out of all its windows and ran out into the darkness from the door when it opened to let some one in. Laura almost jumped out from under the blankets before she remembered that she must never stand up in the wagon when the horses were going.

Pa drove to the church steps and helped them all out. He told them to go in, but they waited in the cold until he had covered Sam and David with their blankets. Then he came, and they all went into the church together.

Laura's mouth fell open and her eyes stretched to look at what she saw. She held Mary's hand tightly and they followed Ma and Pa. They sat down. Then Laura could look with all her might.

Standing in front of the crowded benches was a tree. Laura decided it must be a tree. She could see its trunk and branches. But she had never before seen such a tree.

Where leaves would be in summer, there were clusters and streamers of thin green paper. Thick among them hung little sacks made of pink

mosquito-bar. Laura was almost sure she could see candy in them. From the branches hung packages wrapped in colored paper, red packages and pink packages and yellow packages, all tied with colored string. Silk scarves were draped among them. Red mittens hung by the cord that would go around your neck and keep them from being lost if you were wearing them. A pair of new shoes hung by their heels from a branch. Lavish strings of white popcorn were looped all over this.

Under the tree and leaning against it were all kinds of things. Laura saw a crinkly-bright washboard, a wooden tub, a churn and dasher, a sled made of new boards, a shovel, a long-handled pitchfork.

Laura was too excited to speak. She squeezed Mary's hand tighter and tighter, and she looked up at Ma, wanting so much to know what that was. Ma smiled down at her and answered, "That is a Christmas tree, girls. Do you think it is pretty?"

They could not answer. They nodded while they kept on looking at that wonderful tree. They

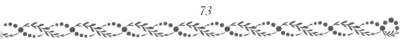

were hardly even surprised to know that this was Christmas, though they had not expected Christmas yet because there was not enough snow. Just then Laura saw the most wonderful thing of all. From a far branch of that tree hung a little fur cape, and a muff to match!

The Reverend Alden was there. He preached about Christmas, but Laura was looking at that tree and she could not hear what he said. Everyone stood up to sing and Laura stood up, but she could not sing. Not a sound would come out of her throat. In the whole world, there couldn't be a store so wonderful to look at as that tree.

After the singing, Mr. Tower and Mr. Beadle began taking things off it, and reading out names. Mrs. Tower and Miss Beadle brought those things down past the benches, and gave them to the person whose name was on them.

Everything on that tree was a Christmas present for somebody!

When Laura knew that, the lamps and people and voices and even the tree began to whirl. They whirled faster, noisier, and more excited. Some one

gave her a pink mosquito-bar bag. It did have candy in it, and a big popcorn ball. Mary had one, too. So did Carrie. Every girl and boy had one. Then Mary had a pair of blue mittens. Then Laura had a red pair.

Ma opened a big package, and there was a warm, big, brown-and-red plaid shawl for her. Pa got a woolly muffler. Then Carrie had a rag doll with a china head. She screamed for joy. Through the laughing and talking and rustling of papers Mr. Beadle and Mr. Tower went on shouting names.

The little fur cape and muff still hung on the tree, and Laura wanted them. She wanted to look at them as long as she could. She wanted to know who got them. They could not be for Nellie Oleson who already had a fur cape.

Laura did not expect anything more. But to Mary came a pretty little booklet with Bible pictures in it, from Mrs. Tower.

Mr. Tower was taking the little fur cape and the muff from the tree. He read a name, but Laura could not hear it through all the joyful noise. She

lost sight of the cape and muff among all the people. They were gone now.

Then to Carrie came a cunning little brown-spotted white china dog. But Carrie's arms and her eyes were full of her doll. So Laura held and stroked and laughed over the sleek little dog.

"Merry Christmas, Laura!" Miss Beadle said, and in Laura's hand she put a beautiful little box. It was made of snow-white, gleaming china. On its top stood a wee, gold-colored teapot and a gold-colored tiny cup in a gold-colored saucer.

The top of the box lifted off. Inside was a nice place to keep a breast-pin, if some day Laura had a breast-pin. Ma said it was a jewel-box.

There had never been such a Christmas as this. It was such a large, rich Christmas, the whole church full of Christmas. There were so many lamps, so many people, so much noise and laughter, and so many happi-nesses in it. Laura felt full and bursting, as if that whole big rich Christmas were inside her, and her mittens and her beautiful jewel-box with the

wee gold cup-and-saucer and teapot, and her candy
and her popcorn ball. And suddenly someone said,
"These are for you, Laura."

Mrs. Tower stood smiling, holding out the little
fur cape and muff.

"For me?" Laura said. "For me?" Then everything else vanished while with both arms she
hugged the soft furs to her.

She hugged them tighter and tighter, trying to
believe they were really hers, that silky-soft little
brown fur cape and the muff.

All around her Christmas went on, but
Laura knew only the softness of those furs.
People were going home. Carrie was standing
on the bench while Ma fastened her coat and
tied her hood more snugly. Ma was saying, "Thank
you so much for the shawl, Brother Alden. It is just
what I needed."

Pa said, "And I thank you for the muffler. It will
feel good when I come to town in the cold."

The Reverend Alden sat down on the bench
and asked, "And does Mary's coat fit?"

Laura had not noticed Mary's coat until then.

Mary had on a new dark-blue coat. It was long, and its sleeves came down to Mary's wrists. Mary buttoned it up, and it fitted.

"And how does this little girl like her furs?" the Reverend Alden smiled. He drew Laura between his knees. He laid the fur cape around her shoulders and fastened it at the throat. He put the cord of the muff around her neck, and her hands went inside the silky muff.

"There!" the Reverend Alden said. "Now my little country girls will be warm when they come to Sunday school."

"What do you say, Laura?" Ma asked, but the Reverend Alden said, "There is no need. The way her eyes are shining is enough."

Laura could not speak. The golden-brown fur cuddled her neck and softly hugged her shoulders. Down her front it hid the threadbare fastenings of her coat. The muff came far up her wrists and hid the shortness of her coat sleeves.

"She's a little brown bird with red trimmings," the Reverend Alden said.

Then Laura laughed. It was true. Her

hair and her coat, her dress and the wonderful furs, were brown. Her hood and mittens and the braid on her dress were red.

"I'll tell my church people back east about our little brown bird," said the Reverend Alden. "You see, when I told them about our church out here, they said they must send a box for the Christmas tree. They all gave things they had. The little girls who sent your furs and Mary's coat needed larger ones."

"Thank you, sir," said Laura. "And please, sir, tell them thank you, too." For when she could speak, her manners were as nice as Mary's.

Then they all said good night and Merry Christmas to the Reverend Alden. Mary was so beautiful in her Christmas coat. Carrie was so pretty on Pa's arm. Pa and Ma were smiling so happily and Laura was all gladness.

Mr. and Mrs. Oleson were going home, too. Mr. Oleson's arms were full of things, and so were Nellie's and Willie's. No wickedness boiled up in Laura now; she only felt a little bit of mean gladness.

"Merry Christmas, Nellie," Laura said. Nellie stared, while Laura walked quietly on, with her hands snuggled deep in the soft muff. Her cape was prettier than Nellie's, and Nellie had no muff.

F ar away from Laura's little log house on the western prairie, Almanzo Wilder is growing up in Malone, New York, learning to help his family work their farm. As Christmastime approaches this year, he has so much to look forward to: the delicious feast of stuffed goose, fresh-baked bread and pumpkin pie, a stocking filled with treats, and a special visit from all his aunts, uncles, and cousins, who are coming to spend Christmas on the Wilder family's farm.

Christmas
for
Farmer Boy

Christmas

FOR A LONG TIME IT SEEMED THAT CHRISTMAS would never come. On Christmas, Uncle Andrew and Aunt Delia, Uncle Wesley and Aunt Lindy, and all the cousins were coming to dinner. It would be the best dinner of the whole year. And a good boy might get something in his stocking. Bad boys found nothing but switches in their stockings on Christmas morning. Almanzo tried to be good for so long that he could hardly stand the strain.

But at last it was the day before Christmas and Alice and Royal and Eliza Jane were home again.

The girls were cleaning the whole house, and Mother was baking. Royal helped Father with the threshing, but Almanzo had to help in the house. He remembered the switch, and tried to be willing and cheerful.

He had to scour the steel knives and forks, and polish the silver. He had to wear an apron around his neck. He took the scouring-brick and scraped a pile of red dust off it, and then with a wet cloth he rubbed the dust up and down on the knives and forks.

The kitchen was full of delicious smells. Newly baked bread was cooling, frosted cakes and cookies and mince pies and pumpkin pies filled the pantry

shelves, cranberries bubbled on the stove. Mother was making dressing for the goose.

Outdoors, the sun was shining on the snow. The icicles twinkled all along the eaves. Far away sleigh-bells faintly jingled, and from the barns came the joyful thud-thud! thud-thud! of the flails. But when all the steel knives and forks were done, Almanzo soberly polished the silver.

Then he had to run to the attic for sage; he had to run down cellar for apples, and upstairs again for onions. He filled the woodbox. He hurried in the cold to fetch water from the pump. He thought maybe he was through, then, anyway for a minute. But no; he had to polish the dining-room side of the stove.

"Do the parlor side yourself, Eliza Jane," Mother said. "Almanzo might spill the blacking."

Almanzo's insides quaked. He knew what would happen if Mother knew about that black splotch, hidden on the parlor wall. He didn't want to get a switch in his Christmas stocking, but he would far rather find a switch there than have Father take him to the woodshed.

That night everyone was tired, and the house was so clean and neat that nobody dared touch anything. After supper Mother put the stuffed, fat goose and the little pig into the heater's oven to roast slowly all night. Father set the dampers and wound the clock. Almanzo and Royal hung clean socks on the back of a chair, and Alice and Eliza Jane hung stockings on the back of another chair.

Then they all took candles and went to bed.

It was still dark when Almanzo woke up. He felt excited, and then he remembered that this was Christmas morning. He jerked back the covers and jumped onto something alive that squirmed. It was Royal. He had forgotten that Royal was there, but he scrambled over him, yelling:

"Christmas! Christmas! Merry Christmas!"

He pulled his trousers over his nightshirt. Royal jumped out of bed and lighted the candle. Almanzo grabbed the candle, and Royal shouted:

"Hi! Leave that be! Where's my pants?"

But Almanzo was already running downstairs. Alice and Eliza Jane were flying from their room,

but Almanzo beat them. He saw his sock hanging all lumpy; he set down the candle and grabbed his sock. The first thing he pulled out was a cap, a boughten cap!

The plaid cloth was machine-woven. So was the lining. Even the sewing was machine-sewing. And the ear-muffs were buttoned over the top.

Almanzo yelled. He had not even hoped for such a cap. He looked at it, inside and out; he felt the cloth and the sleek lining. He put the cap on his head. It was a little large, because he was growing. So he could wear it a long time.

Eliza Jane and Alice were digging into their stockings and squealing, and Royal had a silk muffler. Almanzo thrust his hand into his sock again, and pulled out a nickel's worth of horehound candy. He bit off the end of one stick. The outside melted like maple sugar, but the inside was hard and could be sucked for hours.

Then he pulled out a new pair of mittens. Mother had knit the wrists and backs in a fancy stitch. He pulled out an orange, and he pulled out a little package of dried figs. And he thought that

was all. He thought no boy ever had a better Christmas.

But in the toe of the sock there was still something more. It was small and thin and hard. Almanzo couldn't imagine what it was. He pulled it out, and it was a jack-knife. It had four blades.

Almanzo yelled and yelled. He snapped all the blades open, sharp and shining, and he yelled,

"Alice, look! Look, Royal! Lookee, lookee my jack-knife! Lookee my cap!"

Father's voice came out of the dark bedroom and said:

"Look at the clock."

They all looked at one another. Then Royal held up the candle and they looked at the tall clock. Its hands pointed to half past three.

Even Eliza Jane did not know what to do. They had waked up Father and Mother, an hour and a half before time to get up.

"What time is it?" Father asked.

Almanzo looked at Royal. Royal and Almanzo looked at Eliza Jane. Eliza Jane swallowed, and opened her mouth, but Alice said:

"Merry Christmas, Father! Merry Christmas, Mother! It's—it's—thirty minutes to four, Father."

The clock said, "Tick! Tock! Tick! Tock! Tick!" Then Father chuckled.

Royal opened the dampers of the heater, and Eliza Jane stirred up the kitchen fire and put the kettle on. The house was warm and cosy when Father and Mother got up, and they had a whole hour to spare. There was time to enjoy the presents.

Alice had a gold locket, and Eliza Jane had a pair of garnet earrings. Mother had knitted new lace collars and black lace mitts for them both. Royal had the silk muffler and a fine leather wallet. But Almanzo thought he had the best presents of all. It was a wonderful Christmas.

Then Mother began to hurry, and to hurry everyone else. There were the chores to do, the milk to skim, the new milk to strain and put away, breakfast to eat, vegetables to be peeled, and the whole house must be put in order and everybody dressed up before the company came.

The sun rushed up the sky. Mother was every-where, talking all the time. "Almanzo, wash your

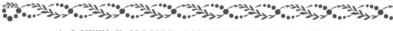

ears! Goodness mercy, Royal, don't stand around underfoot! Eliza Jane, remember you're paring those potatoes, not slicing them, and don't leave so many eyes they can see to jump out of the pot. Count the silver, Alice, and piece it out with the steel knives and forks. The best bleached tablecloths are on the bottom shelf. Mercy on us, look at that clock!"

Sleigh-bells came jingling up the road, and Mother slammed the oven door and ran to change her apron and pin on her brooch; Alice ran downstairs and Eliza Jane ran upstairs, both of them told Almanzo to straighten his collar. Father was calling

Mother to fold his cravat. Then Uncle Wesley's sleigh stopped with a last clash of bells.

Almanzo ran out, whooping, and Father and Mother came behind him, as calm as if they had never hurried in their lives. Frank and Fred and Abner and Mary tumbled out of the sleigh, all bundled up, and before Aunt Lindy had handed Mother the baby, Uncle Andrew's sleigh was coming. The yard was full of boys and the house filled with hoopskirts. The uncles stamped snow off their boots and unwound their mufflers.

Royal and Cousin James drove the sleighs into the Buggy-House; they unhitched the horses and put them in stalls and rubbed down their snowy legs.

Almanzo was wearing his boughten cap, and he showed the cousins his jack-knife. Frank's cap was old now. He had a jack-knife, but it had only three blades.

Then Almanzo showed his cousins Star and Bright, and the little bobsled, and he let them scratch Lucy's fat white back with corncobs. He said they could look at Starlight if they'd be quiet and not scare him.

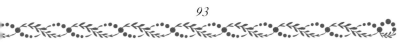

The beautiful colt twitched his tail, and came daintily stepping toward them. Then he tossed his head and shied away from Frank's hand thrust through the bars.

"You leave him be!" Almanzo said.

"I bet you don't dast go in there and get on his back," said Frank.

"I dast, but I got better sense," Almanzo told him. "I know better than to spoil that fine colt."

"How'd it spoil him?" Frank said. "Yah, you're scared he'd hurt you! You're scared of that little bitty colt!"

"I am not scared," said Almanzo. "But Father won't let me."

"I guess I'd do it if I wanted to, if I was you. I guess your father wouldn't know," Frank said.

Almanzo didn't answer, and Frank got up on the bars of the stall.

"You get down off there!" Almanzo said, and he took hold of Frank's leg. "Don't you scare that colt!"

"I'll scare him if I want to," Frank said, kicking. Almanzo hung on. Starlight was running around and around the stall, and Almanzo wanted to yell

for Royal. But he knew that would frighten Starlight even more.

He set his teeth and gave a mighty tug, and Frank came tumbling down. All the horses jumped, and Starlight reared and smashed against the manger.

"I'll lick you for that," Frank said, scrambling up.

"You just try and lick me!" said Almanzo.

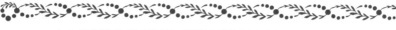

Royal came hurrying from the South Barn. He took Almanzo and Frank by the shoulders and marched them outdoors. Fred and Abner and John came silently after them, and Almanzo's knees wabbled. He was afraid Royal would tell Father.

"Let me catch you boys fooling around those colts again," Royal said, "and I'll tell Father and Uncle Wesley. You'll get the hides thrashed off you."

Royal shook Almanzo so hard that he couldn't tell how hard Royal was shaking Frank. Then he knocked their heads together. Almanzo saw stars.

"Let that teach you to fight. On Christmas Day! For shame!" Royal said.

"I only didn't want him to scare Starlight," Almanzo said.

"Shut up!" said Royal. "Don't be a tattle-tale. Now you behave yourselves or you'll wish you had. Go wash your hands; it's dinner-time."

They all went into the kitchen and washed their hands. Mother and the aunts and the girl cousins were taking up the Christmas dinner. The dining-table had been turned around and pulled

out till it was almost as long as the dining-room, and every inch of it was loaded with good things to eat.

Almanzo bowed his head and shut his eyes tight while Father said the blessing. It was a long blessing, because this was Christmas Day. But at last Almanzo could open his eyes. He sat and silently looked at that table.

He looked at the crisp, crackling little pig lying on the blue platter with an apple in its mouth. He looked at the fat roast goose, the drumsticks sticking up, and the edges of dressing curling out. The sound of Father's knife sharpening on the whetstone made him even hungrier.

He looked at the big bowl of cranberry jelly, and at the fluffy mountain of mashed potatoes with melting butter trickling down it. He looked at the heap of mashed turnips, and the golden baked squash, and the pale fried parsnips.

He swallowed hard and tried not to look anymore. He couldn't help seeing the fried apples'n'onions, and the candied carrots. He couldn't help gazing at the triangles of pie, waiting

by his plate; the spicy pumpkin pie, the melting cream pie, the rich, dark mince oozing from between the mince pie's flaky crusts.

He squeezed his hands together between his knees. He had to sit silent and wait, but he felt aching and hollow inside.

All grown-ups at the head of the table must be served first. They were passing their plates, and talking, and heartlessly laughing. The tender pork fell away in slices under Father's carving-knife. The white breast of the goose went piece by piece from the bare breast-bone. Spoons ate up the clear cranberry jelly, and gouged deep into the mashed potatoes, and ladled away the brown gravies.

Almanzo had to wait to the very last. He was youngest of all, except Abner and the babies, and Abner was company.

At last Almanzo's plate was filled. The first taste made a pleasant feeling inside him, and it grew and grew, while he ate and ate and ate. He ate till he could eat no more, and he felt very good inside. For a while he slowly nibbled bits from his second piece of fruitcake. Then he put the fruity slice in his pocket and went out to play.

Royal and James were choosing sides, to play snow-fort. Royal chose Frank, and James chose Almanzo. When everyone was chosen, they all went to work, rolling snowballs through the deep drifts by the barn. They rolled till the balls were almost as tall as Almanzo; then they rolled them into a wall. They packed snow between them, and made a good fort.

Then each side made its own little snowballs. They breathed on the snow, and squeezed it solid. They made dozens of hard snowballs. When they were ready for the fight, Royal threw a stick into the air and caught it when it came down. James took hold of the stick above Royal's hand, then Royal took hold of it above James' hand, and so on to the end of the stick. James' hand was last, so James' side had the fort.

How the snowballs flew! Almanzo ducked and dodged and yelled, and threw snowballs as fast as he could, till they were all gone. Royal came charging over the wall with all the enemy after him, and Almanzo rose up and grabbed Frank. Headlong

they went into the deep snow, outside the wall, and they rolled over and over, hitting each other as hard as they could.

Almanzo's face was covered with snow and his mouth was full of it, but he hung on to Frank and kept hitting him. Frank got him down, but Almanzo squirmed out from under. Frank's head hit his nose, and it began to bleed. Almanzo didn't care. He was on top of Frank, hitting him as hard as he could in the deep snow. He kept saying, "Holler 'nuff! holler 'nuff!"

Frank grunted and squirmed. He rolled half over, and Almanzo got on top of him. He couldn't stay on top of Frank and hit him, so he bore down with all his weight, and he pushed Frank's face deeper and deeper into the snow. And Frank gasped: "'Nuff!"

Almanzo got up on his knees, and he saw Mother in the doorway of the house. She called:

"Boys! Boys! Stop playing now. It's time to come in and warm."

They were warm. They were hot and panting. But Mother and the aunts thought

the cousins must get warm before they rode home in the cold. They all went tramping in, covered with snow, and Mother held up her hands and exclaimed:

"Mercy on us!"

The grown-ups were in the parlor, but the boys had to stay in the dining-room, so they wouldn't melt on the parlor carpet. They couldn't sit down, because the chairs were covered with blankets and laprobes, warming by the heater. But they ate apples and drank cider, standing around, and Almanzo and Abner went into the pantry and ate bits off the platters.

Then uncles and aunts and the girl cousins put on their wraps, and they brought the sleeping babies from the bedroom, rolled up in shawls. The sleighs came jingling from the barn, and Father and Mother helped tuck in the blankets and laprobes, over the hoopskirts. Everybody called: "Good-by! Good-by!"

The music of the sleigh-bells came back for a little while; then it was gone. Christmas was over.

*T*he Ingalls family has moved to De Smet, in Dakota Territory, and this year the blizzards have been relentless. By Christmastime, so much snow has fallen that no trains can make their way into town. The long, cold months go by, and Laura and her sisters spend their first winter without the traditional holiday celebrations. But when the long winter finally comes to an end in May, springtime in De Smet is glorious, and it feels like the perfect time for Christmas.

Christmas
During
the
Long
Winter

The Christmas Barrel

NEXT DAY THE SECOND TRAIN CAME. After its departing whistle had died away, Pa and Mr. Boast came down the street carrying a barrel between them. They upended it through the doorway and stood it in the middle of the front room.

"Here's that Christmas barrel!" Pa called to Ma.

He brought his hammer and began pulling nails out of the barrel-head, while they all stood around it waiting to see what was in it. Pa took off the barrel-head. Then he lifted away some thick brown paper that covered everything beneath.

Clothes were on top. First Pa drew out a dress

of beautifully fine, dark-blue flannel. The skirt was full pleated and the neat, whaleboned basque was buttoned down the front with cut-steel buttons.

"This is about your size, Caroline," Pa beamed. "Here, take it!" and he reached again into the barrel.

He took out a fluffy, light-blue fascinator for Mary, and some warm flannel underthings. He took out a pair of black leather shoes that exactly fitted Laura. He took out five pairs of white woolen stockings, machine-knit. They were much finer and thinner than home-knit ones.

Then he took out a warm, brown coat, a little large for Carrie, but it would fit her next winter. And he took out a red hood and mittens to go with it.

Next came a silk shawl!

"Oh, Mary!" Laura said. "The most beautiful thing—a shawl made of silk! It is dove-colored,

with fine stripes of green and rose and black and the richest, deep fringe with all those colors shimmering in it. Feel how soft and rich and heavy the silk is," and she put a corner of the shawl in Mary's hand.

"Oh, lovely!" Mary breathed.

"Who gets this shawl?" Pa asked, and they all said, "Ma!" Such a beautiful shawl was for Ma, of course. Pa laid it on her arm, and it was like her, so soft and yet firm and well-wearing, with the fine, bright colors in it.

"We will all take turns wearing it," Ma said. "And Mary shall take it with her when she goes to college."

"What is there for you, Pa?" Laura asked jealously. For Pa there were two fine, white shirts, and a dark brown plush cap.

"That isn't all," said Pa, and he lifted out of the barrel one, two little dresses. One was blue flannel, one was green-and-rose plaid. They were too small for Carrie and too big for Grace, but Grace would grow to fit them. Then were was an A-B-C book printed on cloth, and a small, shiny Mother Goose

book of the smoothest paper, with a colored picture on the cover.

There was a pasteboard box full of bright-colored yarns and another box filled with embroidery silks and sheets of perforated thin cardboard, silver-colored and gold-colored. Ma gave both boxes to Laura, saying, "You gave away the pretty things you had made. Now here are some lovely things for you to work with."

Laura was so happy that she couldn't say a word. The delicate silks caught on the roughness of her fingers, scarred from twisting hay, but the beautiful colors sang together like music, and her fingers would grow smooth again so that she could embroider on the fine, thin silver and gold.

"Now I wonder what this can be?" Pa said, as he lifted from the very bottom of the barrel something bulky and lumpy that was wrapped around and around with thick brown paper.

"Je-ru-salem crickets!" he exclaimed. "If it isn't our Christmas turkey, still frozen solid!"

He held the great turkey up where all could see. "And fat! Fifteen pounds or I miss my guess."

And as he let the mass of brown paper fall, it thumped on the floor and out of it rolled several cranberries.

"And if here isn't a package of cranberries to go with it!" said Pa.

Carrie shrieked with delight. Mary clasped her hands and said, "Oh my!" But Ma asked, "Did the groceries come for the stores, Charles?"

"Yes, sugar and flour and dried fruit and meat— oh, everything anybody needs," Pa answered.

"Well then, Mr. Boast, you bring Mrs. Boast day after tomorrow," Ma said. "Come as early as you can and we will celebrate the springtime with a Christmas dinner."

"That's the ticket!" Pa shouted, while Mr. Boast threw back his head and the room filled with his ringing laugh. They all joined in, for no one could help laughing when Mr. Boast did.

"We'll come! You bet we'll come!" Mr. Boast chortled. "Christmas dinner in May! That will be great, to feast after a winter of darn near fasting! I'll hurry home and tell Ellie."

Christmas in May

PA BOUGHT GROCERIES THAT AFTERNOON. It was wonderful to see him coming in with armfuls of packages, wonderful to see a whole sack of white flour, sugar, dried apples, soda crackers, and cheese. The kerosene can was full. How happy Laura was to fill the lamp, polish the chimney, and trim the wick. At suppertime the light shone through the clear glass onto the red-checked tablecloth and the white biscuits, the warmed up potatoes, and the platter of fried salt pork.

With yeast cakes, Ma set the sponge for light bread that night, and she put the dried apples to soak for pies.

Laura did not need to be called next morning. She was up at dawn, and all day she helped Ma bake and stew and boil the good things for next day's Christmas dinner.

Early that morning Ma added water and flour to the bread sponge and set it to rise again. Laura and Carrie picked over the cranberries and washed them. Ma stewed them with sugar until they were a mass of crimson jelly.

Laura and Carrie carefully picked dried raisins from their long stems and carefully took the seeds out of each one. Ma stewed the dried apples, mixed the raisins with them, and made pies.

"It seems strange to have everything one could want to work with," said Ma. "Now I have cream of tartar and plenty of saleratus, I shall make a cake."

All day long the kitchen smelled of good things, and when night came the cupboard held large brown-crusted loaves of white bread, a sugar-frosted loaf of cake, three crisp-crusted pies, and the jellied cranberries.

"I wish we could eat them now," Mary said.

"Seems like I can't wait till tomorrow."

"I'm waiting for the turkey first," said Laura, "and you may have sage in the stuffing, Mary."

She sounded generous but Mary laughed at her. "That's only because there aren't any onions for you to use!"

"Now, girls, don't get impatient," Ma begged them. "We will have a loaf of light bread and some of the cranberry sauce for supper."

So the Christmas feasting was begun the night before.

It seemed too bad to lose any of that happy time in sleep. Still, sleeping was the quickest way to tomorrow morning. It was no time at all, after Laura's eyes closed, till Ma was calling her and tomorrow was today.

What a hurrying there was! Breakfast was soon over, then while Laura and Carrie cleared the table and washed the dishes, Ma prepared the big turkey for roasting and mixed the bread-stuffing for it.

The May morning was warm and the wind from the prairie smelled of springtime. Doors were open and both rooms could be used once more. Going in

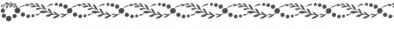

and out of the large front room whenever she wanted to, gave Laura a spacious and rested feeling, as if she could never be cross again.

Ma had already put the rocking chairs by the front windows to get them out of her way in the kitchen. Now the turkey was in the oven, and Mary helped Laura draw the table into the middle of the front room. Mary raised its drop-leaves and spread smoothly over it the white tablecloth that Laura brought her. Then Laura brought the dishes from the cupboard and Mary placed them around the table.

Carrie was peeling potatoes and Grace was running races with herself the length of both rooms.

Ma brought the glass bowl filled with glowing cranberry jelly. She set it in the middle of the white tablecloth and they all admired the effect.

"We do need some butter to go with the light bread, though," Ma said.

"Never mind, Caroline," said Pa. "There's tar-paper at the lumberyard now. I'll soon fix up the shanty and we'll move out to the homestead in a few days."

The roasting turkey was filling the house with scents that made their mouths water. The potatoes were boiling and Ma was putting the coffee on when Mr. and Mrs. Boast came walking in.

"For the last mile, I've been following my nose to that turkey!" Mr. Boast declared.

"I was thinking more of seeing the folks, Robert, than of anything to eat," Mrs. Boast chided him. She was thin and the lovely rosy color was gone from her cheeks, but she was the same darling Mrs. Boast, with the same laughing black-fringed blue eyes and the same dark hair curling under the same brown hood. She shook hands warmly with Ma and Mary and Laura and stooped down to draw Carrie and Grace close in her arms while she spoke to them.

"Come into the front room and take off your things, Mrs. Boast," Ma urged her. "It is good to see you again after so long. Now you rest in the rocking chair and visit with Mary while I finish up dinner."

"Let me help you," Mrs. Boast asked, but Ma said she must be tired after her long walk and

everything was nearly ready.

"Laura and I will soon have dinner on the table," said Ma, turning quickly back to the kitchen. She ran against Pa in her haste.

"We better make ourselves scarce, Boast," said Pa. "Come along, and I'll show you the *Pioneer Press* I got this morning."

"It will be good to see a newspaper again," Mr. Boast agreed eagerly. So the kitchen was left to the cooks.

"Get the big platter to put the turkey on," Ma said, as she lifted the heavy dripping-pan out of the oven.

Laura turned to the cupboard and saw on the shelf a package that had not been there before.

 "What's that, Ma?" she asked.

"I don't know. Look and see," Ma told her, and Laura undid the paper. There on a small plate was a ball of butter.

"Butter! It's butter!" she almost shouted.

They heard Mrs. Boast laugh. "Just a little Christmas present!" she called.

Pa and Mary and Carrie exclaimed aloud in

delight and Grace squealed long and shrill while Laura carried the butter to the table. Then she hurried back to slide the big platter carefully beneath the turkey as Ma raised it from the dripping-pan.

While Ma made the gravy Laura mashed the potatoes. There was no milk, but Ma said, "Leave a very little of the boiling water in, and after you mash them beat them extra hard with the big spoon."

The potatoes turned out white and fluffy, though not with the flavor that plenty of hot milk and butter would have given them.

When all the chairs were drawn up to the well-filled table, Ma looked at Pa and every head bowed.

"Lord, we thank Thee for all Thy bounty." That was all Pa said, but it seemed to say everything.

"The table looks some different from what it did a few days ago," Pa said as he heaped Mrs. Boast's plate with turkey and stuffing and potatoes and a large spoonful of cranberries. And as he went

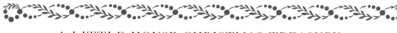

on filling the plates he added, "It has been a long winter."

"And a hard one," said Mr. Boast.

"It is a wonder how we all kept well and came through it," Mrs. Boast said.

While Mr. and Mrs. Boast told how they had worked and contrived through that long winter, all alone in the blizzard-bound shanty on their claim, Ma poured the coffee and Pa's tea. She passed the bread and the butter and the gravy and reminded Pa to refill the plates.

When every plate had been emptied a second time Ma refilled the cups and Laura brought on the pies and the cake.

They sat a long time at the table, talking of the winter that was past and the summer to come. Ma said she could hardly wait to get back to the homestead. The wet, muddy roads were the difficulty now, but Pa and Mr. Boast agreed that they would dry out before long. The Boasts were glad that they had wintered on their claim and didn't have to move back to it now.

At last they all left the table. Laura brought the

red-bordered table cover and Carrie helped her to spread it to cover neatly out of sight the food and the empty dishes. Then they joined the others by the sunny window.

Pa stretched his arms above his head. He opened and closed his hands and stretched his fingers wide, then ran them through his hair till it all stood on end.

"I believe this warm weather has taken the stiffness out of my fingers," he said. "If you will bring me the fiddle, Laura, I'll see what I can do."

Laura brought the fiddle-box and stood close by while Pa lifted the fiddle out of its nest. He thumbed the strings and tightened the keys as he listened. Then he rosined the bow and drew it across the strings.

A few clear, true notes softly sounded. The lump in Laura's throat almost choked her.

Pa played a few bars and said, "This is a new song I learned last fall, the time we went to Volga to clear the tracks. You hum the tenor along with the fiddle, Boast, while I sing it through the first

time. A few times over, and you'll all pick up the words."

They all gathered around him to listen while he played again the opening bars. Then Mr. Boast's tenor joined the fiddle's voice and Pa's voice singing:

"This life is a difficult riddle,
  For how many people we see
  With faces as long as a fiddle
  That ought to be shining with glee.
  I am sure in this world there are plenty
  Of good things enough for us all
  And yet there's not one out of twenty
  But thinks that his share is too small.

"Then what is the use of repining,
  For where there's a will, there's a way,
  And tomorrow the sun may be shining,
  Although it is cloudy today.

"Do you think that by sitting and sighing
  You'll ever obtain all you want?

It's cowards alone that are crying
And foolishly saying, 'I can't!'
It is only by plodding and striving
And laboring up the steep hill
Of life, that you'll ever be thriving
Which you'll do if you've only the will."

They were all humming the melody now and when the chorus came again, Mrs. Boast's alto, Ma's contralto, and Mary's sweet soprano joined Mr. Boast's tenor and Pa's rich bass, singing the words, and Laura sang, too, soprano:

"Then what is the use of repining,
For where there's a will, there's a way,
And tomorrow the sun may be shining,
Although it is cloudy today."

And as they sang, the fear and the suffering of the long winter seemed to rise like a dark cloud and float away on the music. Spring had come. The sun was shining warm, the winds were soft, and the green grass growing.

O n Christmas Eve, a storm
blows in, and the Ingalls family
must celebrate the holidays at home.
Laura is all grown up now and engaged
to Almanzo Wilder. Laura, Carrie, and
Grace scurry about to prepare for the
festivities, filling bags with candy and
enjoying the music from Pa's fiddle.
But somehow Christmas just doesn't feel
the same with Mary away at a school for
the blind and Almanzo all the way in
New York. When a surprise visitor knocks
on the door, Laura receives the most special
gift she could ever have hoped for.

Merry Christmas, Laura!

Christmas
in the
Golden Years

The Night Before Christmas

ON CHRISTMAS EVE AGAIN, THERE WAS A Christmas tree at the church in town. In good time, the Christmas box had gone to Mary, and the house was full of Christmas secrets as the girls hid from each other to wrap the presents for the Christmas tree. But at ten o'clock that morning, snow began to fall.

Still it seemed that it might be possible to go to the Christmas tree. All the afternoon Grace watched from the window, and once or twice the wind moderated. By suppertime, however, it was howling at the eaves, and the air

was thick with flying snow.

"It's too dangerous to risk it," Pa said. It was a straight wind, blowing steadily, but you never could tell; it might turn into a blizzard while the people were in the church.

No plans had been made for Christmas Eve at home, so everyone had much to do. In the kitchen Laura was popping corn in the iron kettle set into a hole of the stove top from which she had removed the stove lid. She put a handful of salt into the kettle; when it was hot she put in a handful of popcorn. With a long-handled spoon she stirred it, while with the other hand she held the kettle's cover to keep the corn from flying out as it popped. When it stopped popping she dropped in

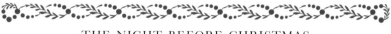

another handful of corn and kept on stirring, but now she need not hold the cover, for the popped white kernels stayed on top and kept the popping kernels from jumping out of the kettle.

Ma was boiling molasses in a pan. When Laura's kettle was full of popped corn, Ma dipped some into a large pan, poured a thin trickle of the boiling molasses over it, and then buttering her hands, she deftly squeezed handfuls of it into pop-corn balls. Laura kept popping corn and Ma made it into balls until the large dishpan was heaped with their sweet crispness.

In the sitting room Carrie and Grace made little bags of pink mosquito netting, left over last summer from the screen door. They filled the bags with Christmas candy that Pa had brought from town that week.

"It's lucky I thought we'd want more candy than we'd likely get at the Christmas tree," Pa took credit to himself.

"Oh!" Carrie discovered. "We've made one bag too many. Grace miscounted."

"I did not!" Grace cried.

"Grace," Ma said.

"I am not contradicting!" cried Grace.

"Grace," said Pa.

Grace gulped. "Pa," she said. "I didn't count wrong. I guess I can count five! There was candy enough for another one, and it looks pretty in the pink bag."

"So it does, and it is nice to have an extra one. We haven't always been so lucky," Pa told her.

Laura remembered the Christmas on the Verdigris River in Indian Territory, when Mr. Edwards had walked eighty miles to bring her and Mary each one stick of candy. Wherever he was tonight, she wished him as much happiness as he had brought them. She remembered the Christmas Eve on Plum Creek in Minnesota, when Pa had been lost in the blizzard and they feared he would never come back. He had eaten the Christmas candy while he lay sheltered three days under the creek bank. Now here they were, in the snug warm house, with plenty of candy and other good things.

Yet now she wished that Mary were there, and

she was trying not to think of Almanzo. When he first went away, letters had come from him often; then they had come regularly. Now for three weeks there had been no letter. He was at home, Laura thought, meeting his old friends and the girls he used to know. Springtime was four months away. He might forget her, or wish that he had not given her the ring that sparkled on her finger.

Pa broke into her thoughts. "Bring me the fiddle, Laura. Let's have a little music before we begin on these good things."

She brought him the fiddle box and he tuned the fiddle and resined the bow. "What shall I play?"

"Play Mary's song first," Laura answered. "Perhaps she is thinking of us."

Pa drew the bow across the strings and he and the fiddle sang:

"Ye banks and braes and streams around
The castle of Montgomery,
Green be your woods and fair your flowers,
Your waters never drumlie;

There summer first unfolds her robes
And there the langest tarry,
For there I took the last fareweel
Of my sweet Highland Mary."

One Scots song reminded Pa of another, and with the fiddle he sang:

"My heart is sair, I dare na tell,
My heart is sair for somebody.
Oh! I could wake a winter night,
A' for the sake o' somebody."

Ma sat in her rocking chair beside the heater, and Carrie and Grace were snug in the window seat, but Laura moved restlessly around the room.

The fiddle sang a wandering tune of its own that made her remember June's wild roses. Then it caught up another tune to blend with Pa's voice.

"When marshalled on the mighty plane,
The glittering hosts bestud the sky

One star alone of all the train
Can catch the sinner's wandering eye.
It was my light, my guide, my all,
It bade my dark forebodings cease,
And through the storm and dangers thrall
It led me to the port of peace.
Now safely moored, my perils o'er,
I'll sing, first in night's diadem
Forever and forever more,
The Star—the Star of Bethlehem."

Grace said softly, "The Christmas star."

The fiddle sang to itself again while Pa cocked his head, listening. "The wind is rising," he said. "Good thing we stayed home."

Then the fiddle began to laugh and Pa's voice laughed as he sang,

"Oh, do not stand so long outside,
Why need you be so shy?
The people's ears are open, John,
As they are passing by!

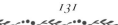

You can not tell what they may think
They've said strange things before
And if you wish to talk awhile,
Come in and shut the door!
Come in! Come in! Come in!"

Laura looked at Pa in amazement as he sang so loudly, looking at the door, "Come in! Come in! Come . . ."

Someone knocked at the door. Pa nodded to Laura to go to the door, while he ended the song. "Come in and shut the door!"

A gust of wind swirled snow into the room when Laura opened the door; it blinded her for a moment and when she could see she could not believe her eyes. The wind whirled snow around Almanzo as, speechless, she stood holding the door open.

"Come in!" Pa called. "Come in and shut the door!" Shivering, he laid the fiddle in its box and put more coal on the fire. "That wind blows the cold into a fellow's bones," he said. "What about your team?"

"I drove Prince, and I put him in the stable beside Lady," Almanzo answered, as he shook the snow from his overcoat and hung it with his cap on the polished buffalo horns fastened to the wall near the door, while Ma rose from her chair to greet him.

Laura had retreated to the other end of the room, beside Carrie and Grace. When Almanzo looked toward them, Grace said, "I made an extra bag of candy."

"And I brought some oranges," Almanzo answered, taking a paper bag from his overcoat pocket. "I have a package with Laura's name on it, too, but isn't she going speak to me?"

"I can't believe it is you," Laura murmured. "You said you would be gone all winter."

"I decided I didn't want to stay away so long, and as you will speak to me, here is your Christmas gift."

"Come, Charles, put the fiddle away," said Ma. "Carrie and Grace, help me bring in the popcorn balls."

Laura opened the small package that Almanzo gave her. The white paper unfolded; there was a

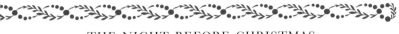

white box inside. She lifted its lid. There in a nest of soft white cotton lay a gold bar pin. On its flat surface was etched a little house, and before it along the bar lay a tiny lake, and a spray of grasses and leaves.

"Oh, it is beautiful," she breathed. "Thank you!"

"Can't you thank a fellow better than that?" he asked, and then he put his arms around her while Laura kissed him and whispered, "I am glad you came back."

Pa came from the kitchen bringing a hodful of coal and Ma followed. Carrie brought in the pan of popcorn balls and Grace gave everyone a bag of candy.

While they ate the sweets, Almanzo told of driving all day in the cold winds and camping on the open prairie with no house nor shelter near, as he and Royal drove south into Nebraska. He told of seeing the beautiful capital building at Omaha; of muddy roads when they turned east into Iowa, where the farmers were burning their corn for fuel because they could not sell it for as much as

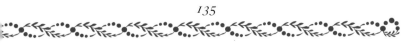

twenty-five cents a bushel. He told of seeing the Iowa state capital at Des Moines; of rivers in flood that they crossed in Iowa and Missouri, until when faced with the Missouri River they turned north again.

So with interesting talk the evening sped by until the old clock struck twelve.

"Merry Christmas!" Ma said, rising from her chair, and "Merry Christmas!" everyone answered.

Almanzo put on his overcoat, his cap and mittens, said good night, and went out into the storm. Faintly the sleigh bells rang as he passed the house on his way home.

"Did you hear them before?" Laura asked Pa.

"Yes, and nobody was ever asked to come in oftener than he was," said Pa. "I suppose he couldn't hear me in the storm."

"Come, come, girls," Ma said. "If you don't get to sleep soon, Santa Claus will have no chance to fill the stockings."

In the morning, there would be all the surprises from the stockings, and at noon there would be the special Christmas feast, with a big fat hen

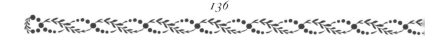

stuffed and roasted, brown and juicy, and Almanzo would be there, for Ma had asked him to Christmas dinner. The wind was blowing hard, but it had not the shriek and howl of a blizzard wind, so probably he would be able to come tomorrow.

"Oh, Laura!" Carrie said, as Laura blew out the lamp in the bedroom. "Isn't this the nicest Christmas! Do Christmases get better all the time?"

"Yes," Laura said. "They do.

Jingle Bells

Lively

Dash-ing through the snow in a one hoss o-pen sleigh,
O'er the fields we go, Laugh-ing all the way. Bells on bob-tail
ring. They're mak-ing spir-its bright. What fun it is to
ride and sing a sleigh-ing song to - night! Jin-gle bells,
jin-gle bells, jin-gle all the way. Oh what fun it
is to ride in a one hoss o-pen sleigh!___ Jin-gle bells,
jin-gle bells, jin-gle all the way. Oh what fun it
is to ride in a one hoss o-pen sleigh. _____